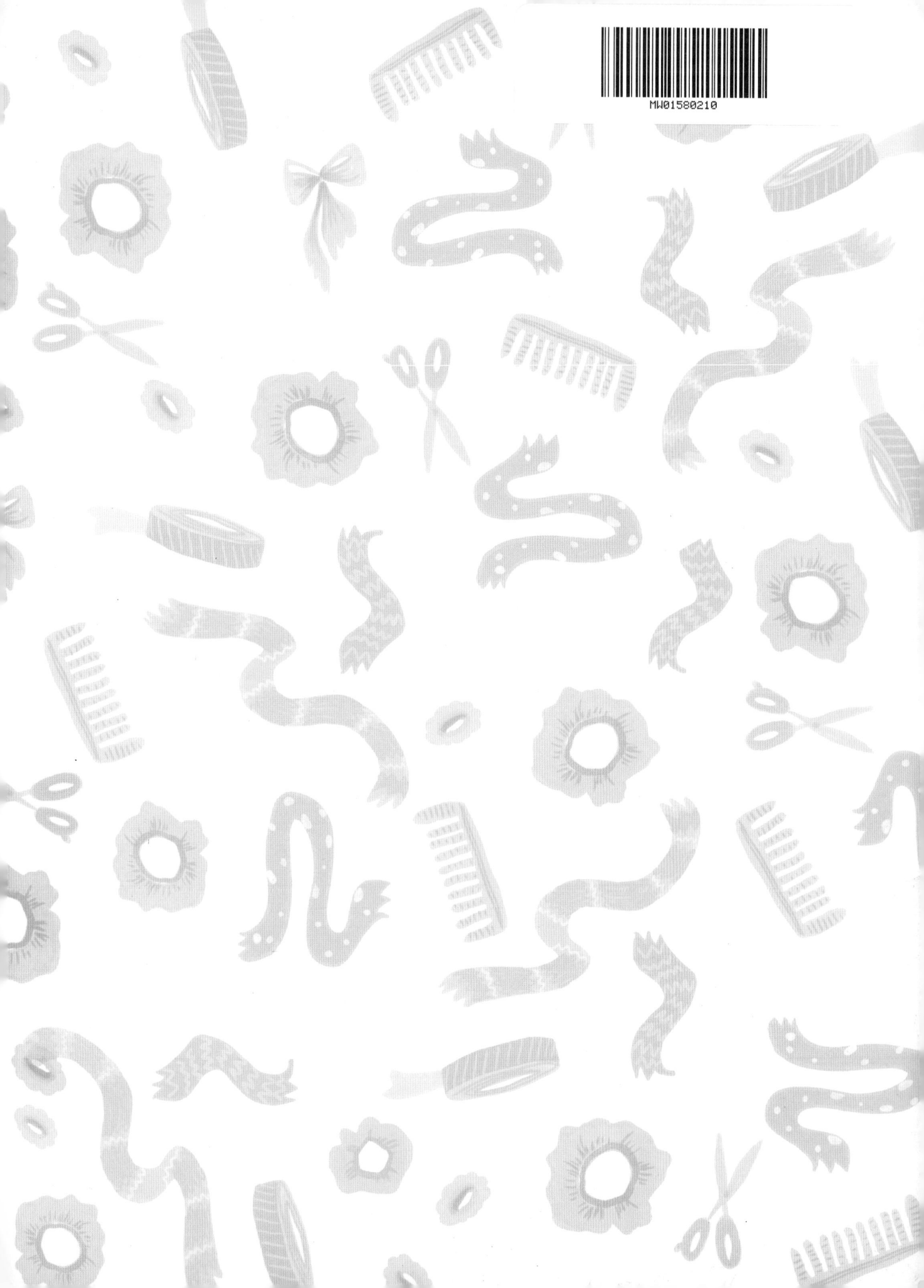

MODERN MARIGOLD BOOKS

Shreya's Very Own Style

Written by Suhani Parikh

Illustrated by Lovyaa Garg

Shreya's Very Own Style © Copyright 2020 by Suhani Parikh. All rights reserved. No part of this book may be reproduced in any form whatsoever, by photography or xerography or by any other means, by broadcast or transmission, by translation into any kind of language, nor by recording electronically or otherwise, without permission in writing from the author, except by a reviewer, who may quote brief passages in critical articles or reviews.

This is a work of fiction. Names, characters, places, and incidents are either the products of the author's imagination or are used in a fictitious manner, and any resemblance to actual persons, living or dead, businesses, events, or locales is purely coincidental.

Edited by Jenny Bowman and Amy Maranville
Illustrated by Lovyaa Garg

ISBN 13: 978-1-7350319-0-3
Library of Congress Catalog Number: 2020908272
Printed in China
First Printing: 2020
24 23 22 21 20   5 4 3 2 1

Book design and typesetting by Tejas Soni.
Cabrito Norm
Smoothy Regular

MODERN MARIGOLD BOOKS

Contact Suhani Parikh at www.raisemarigolds.com for school visits, speaking engagements, book club discussions, freelance writing projects, and interviews.

FSC
www.fsc.org
MIX
Paper from responsible sources
FSC® C129886

For my parents, who always encouraged me to look within and supported my every passion.

Dear R.M., thank you for pushing me to find the voice of my past.
— S.P

For all children, you are incredible exactly as you are.
— L.G.

WHAT IS ALOPECIA AREATA?

Alopecia areata is a common auto-immune disorder that causes unpredictable hair loss on the head, face and other areas of the body.

For more information and resources, please visit
www.raisemarigolds.com/alopecia

Shreya was a whiz at learning things.

larger-than-life things,

and even simple, little things.

She loved learning it all.

But the one thing she could
never quite seem to figure out...

was what else to do with her hair.

Her hair was a little different.

It was thinner than her friends' hair and she could only style it in one way so none of the patches on her head would show.

The patches with no hair at all.

Her family always said,

"Your hair is just one part of everything that makes up who you are."

"But it's a part of me that everyone can see!" Shreya would always reply.

No, it was better to keep the patches covered. After all, what would she say if someone asked her, "Shreya, what happened to your hair?"

Now, if only those pesky strands of hair would stay off of her face.

Ooo a soccer ball?!

With her hair swooped over to one side, Shreya walked onto the field.

She dodged,

dribbled,

and dashed.

She tackled, trapped, and tricked.

She scored the winning goal for her soccer team. Shreya felt like a champion as she lifted the trophy over her head.

But then she spotted her friend Leena's long, ribbon-wrapped ponytail dancing in the breeze.

I wish I could have a ribbon-wrapped ponytail like that, she thought to herself.

Suddenly, the golden trophy didn't sparkle as brightly as it did a moment before.

Shreya didn't feel like celebrating anymore.

Ooo a science fair?!

With her hair swooped over to one side, Shreya took her place behind her table.

She tinkered,

tested,

and tweaked.

She prepared, presented, and placed.

She won first prize at the science fair.

Shreya felt so cool as her teacher placed a gold medal around her neck.

But then she saw the perfect bun that kept all the hair off of her friend Alisha's face.

Shreya waved away a pesky strand of hair and thought,

I wish I could tie my hair in a bun.

Shreya suddenly went from feeling cool to feeling cold. She wished she had a hat to wear.

Ooo a Diwali show?!

DIWALI

With her hair swooped over to one side, Shreya walked onto the stage. She dipped, dove, and dazzled.

She smiled, stepped,

and spun.

BRAVO!

Shreya felt like a star, bowing before a sea of clapping hands.

Just then, her eyes fell on her friend Sona's long, gem-lined braid, ending in a spray of colorful tassels.

Shreya patted her own simple hairstyle and wondered what would happen if she lined her hair with gems.

No, the last thing I need is everyone looking at my head, Shreya thought.

Suddenly, Shreya didn't want to be on stage anymore.

She felt like hiding.

She woke up the next morning feeling glum. As she walked to school, all she could think about were ribbon-wrapped ponytails, perfect buns, and gem-lined braids. All those things would never be a part of who she was.

At school, she went to her cubby and to her surprise, she saw four small pieces of paper. What could these be?

Then she remembered…

These must be notes of kindness! But what could they possibly say? What could others have noticed about her?

She slowly opened each one.

While she had been worrying that people would see something wrong, her friends were focused on everything she was doing right. Even though she didn't have her friends' hairstyles, she did have her own style after all.

"There is nothing I can't do," Shreya whispered to herself.

She went home that afternoon feeling determined. She knew it was time to do something about those pesky strands of hair.

She pulled her hair back in a ponytail. No. She turned the ponytail into a small bun. No. She added some clips, but no. . . none of these would work. She needed a style of her very own. So she started thinking. . .

She thought about how hard she had worked all summer long learning how to kick a soccer ball just right to send it straight into the goal.

She thought about how many hours she had spent working on her science experiment.

And she thought about how she had perfected each and every step of her dance for the show.

The next day, Shreya went to school with a new hairstyle.

I love your HAIR, Shreya!

THAT'S the PRETTIEST HEADBAND I've ever seen!

But what HAPPENED to your HAIR?

Uh-oh.

Her friends did notice.

Shreya took a deep breath. She was nervous. But then she remembered how kind her friends had been. How their notes showed all the things they loved about her.

"Well, I have alopecia so my hair is a little different than yours. I have some spots like these where I have no hair at all," she said nervously.

"That's ok! We all have different hair!" Alicia said.

Shreya blinked in surprise. Alicia was right.

For the first time, Shreya felt not one pesky strand of hair on her face. Instead, she felt proud like a champion, cool like a scientist, and bright like a star.

Shreya's hair was just a part of who she was. . . and all of her was pretty great.

Dear readers,

My journey with alopecia areata began at the age of four. It was an experience that shaped the way I view the world, myself, and how I'm now raising my daughters.

Despite being familiar with alopecia-my father and my aunt both have it, as well-losing my hair was incredibly difficult for me. It was hard on my parents, too. They felt powerless against this condition. But they did find a way to help me: they reminded me every day that I was more than the hair on my head. I'm forever grateful to them for helping me to see beyond the things I cannot change.

It is my hope that this book becomes a conversation starter and a resource, not just for families who are experiencing alopecia, but for all families. I hope that this book helps spread awareness of this condition, and shows that alopecia (or any condition, really) does not take away from the person, but instead adds to their beautiful uniqueness.

To those who have alopecia, whether you choose to wear a smooth head, your natural hair, or a wig because you love long hair, that is up to you. But never forget, it's the person you are inside that matters. **After all, your hair is just one part of everything that makes up who you are.**

With the most love,
Suhani

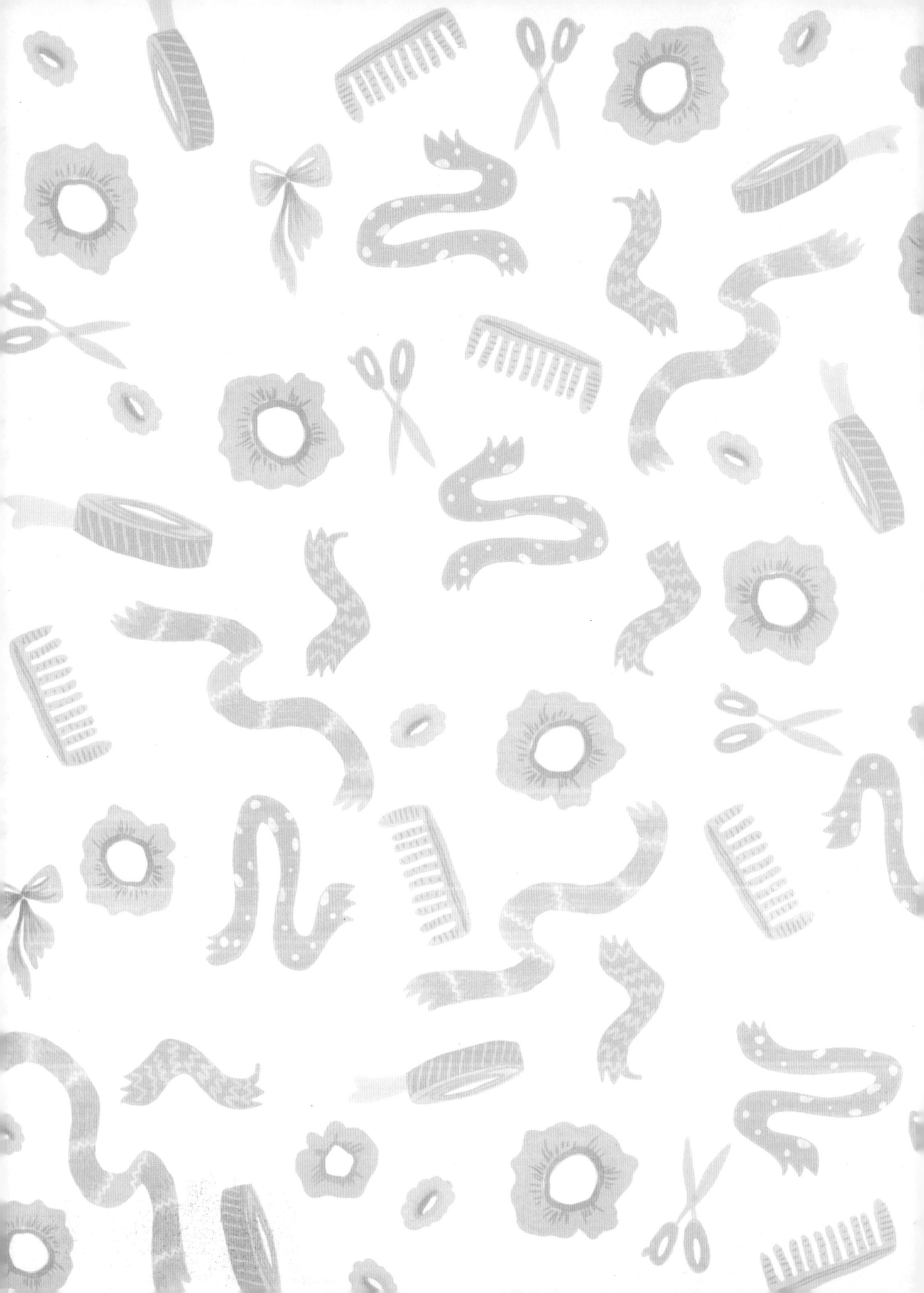